Scratch and Sniff

Margaret Ryan

Illustrated by Nathan Reed

BLOOMSBURY EDUCATION

LONDON OXFORD NEW YORK NEW DELHI SYDNEY

BLOOMSBURY EDUCATION
Bloomsbury Publishing Plc
50 Bedford Square, London, WC1B 3DP, UK

29 Earlsfort Terrace, Dublin 2, Ireland

BLOOMSBURY, BLOOMSBURY EDUCATION and the Diana logo are trademarks of
Bloomsbury Publishing Plc

First published in Great Britain 2006 by A&C Black, an imprint of Bloomsbury
Publishing Plc
This edition published in Great Britain 2021 by Bloomsbury Publishing Plc

A catalogue record for this book is available from the British Library

ISBN: PB: 978-1-4729-8967-3; ePDF: 978-1-4729-8965-9; ePub: 978-1-4729-8966-6

2 4 6 8 10 9 7 5 3 1

Printed and bound in in the UK by CPI Group Ltd, CR0 4YY

MIX
Paper from
responsible sources
FSC® C020471

To find out more about our authors and books visit www.bloomsbury.com and sign up
for our newsletters

Contents

For Tabitha with love

Chapter One

Scratch and Sniff were curled up in the kitchen of Corner Cottage, trying to have a lie-in. But it wasn't easy. Police Constable Penny Penrose was late for work again.

"Has anyone seen my bicycle clips?" she asked.

Scratch scratched, then wandered over to the kitchen door and barked.

"Well done, Scratch," said Penny.
She removed the bicycle clips from
the door handle and put them on.
Then she looked around again.

"Has anyone seen my bicycle
helmet?"

Sniff sniffed, then waddled
underneath the kitchen table
and barked.

"Well done, Sniff," said Penny. She picked up the helmet and put it on. "Now, you two eat up your breakfast and I'll see you later." Then she hurried outside, jumped on her old bike, and pedalled off to the police station.

Scratch yawned and scratched. Sniff yawned and sniffed.

"Shall we stroll over and
check out the food bowls, Sniff?"
said Scratch.

"Good idea, Scratch," said Sniff.
But it wasn't.

"Yuk!" said Scratch. "Dried food
pellets again."

"What does Penny think we are?"
asked Sniff. "Budgies?"

Scratch shook her shaggy, collie head. Sniff rippled his sleek, dachshund body.

It was time for some proper food, they agreed, and headed out through the dog flap to Mrs Pudding's cake shop.

Mrs Pudding was piling up trays with some home baking when they arrived.

"Good morning," she smiled. "Your usual, is it?"

Scratch and Sniff barked and wagged their tails, and then the two of them settled down outside the shop to enjoy their custard buns. They had just got to the squidgy bit in the middle when...

NEE-NAW! NEE-NAW!

Lights flashed, tyres screeched and Sergeant Snide roared past in his police car.

"Looks like Snidey's on a case," said Scratch.

"That he'll probably bungle again," said Sniff. "Let's go and see Penny."

The dogs bounded along the road to the police station.

Penny was standing outside, surrounded by traffic cones.

"I thought you two might turn up," she said. "Inspector Hector's just told me there's been a robbery at Doogood's furniture store. As usual, Sergeant Snide's gone off to investigate by himself. He's left me here to count traffic cones. It's not fair!"

Scratch and Sniff looked at each other. Perhaps they could help Penny solve the crime.

"Looks like a case for the doggy Secret Service," said Scratch.

"Let's take the short cut to Doogood's furniture store and do some investigating ourselves," said Sniff.

Chapter Two

The dogs headed off down
neglected lanes and alleyways.

They dodged dirty dustbins,
leapt over litter, and outran cranky
cats till they arrived opposite
Doogood's furniture store.

They were just in time to see
Sergeant Snide march up to the
entrance of the shop, where the
manager was waiting.

"I am Sergeant Snide," he
bellowed, "and I can spot a crook
a mile away. Take me to the crime
scene immediately."

"Certainly," said the manager. "Come this way."

Scratch and Sniff looked at each other.

"While the great detective is busy inside, shall we look around outside?" asked Scratch.

"Good idea," nodded Sniff. "We might be able to sniff out a few clues."

"We mustn't be seen, though," said Scratch. "I'll slither along on my belly."

"Mine nearly touches the ground anyway," said Sniff, a sausage dog.

The dogs sneaked past the shop window and slipped round the corner to the back of the store. A large van was parked there. It had DOOGOOD'S FURNITURE written on the side.

Suddenly a door opened and two people in brown overalls came out carrying a sofa. They puffed and panted as they heaved it into the back of the van.

"That's strange," whispered Scratch. "Those two must work at Doogood's. But Snidey shouldn't be letting anyone go. He should be keeping them all inside for questioning."

"Snidey's brains are in his boots," muttered Sniff. "Let's take a closer look."

The dogs edged towards the van. They were just in time to hear the taller of the two hiss: "Did you stash the money away safely, Bernie?"

"Stuffed it in the middle cushion, Stan," Bernie replied.

"That sergeant was a real idiot," they laughed, as they climbed into the cab and started the engine.

"They're the robbers!" gasped Scratch, "and they're getting away with the money!"

"We must do something," said Sniff.

Scratch and Sniff looked at each other.

"Cones!" they both barked.

Chapter Three

Scratch and Sniff headed back
down neglected lanes and alleyways.
They outran cranky cats, leapt over
litter, and dodged dirty dustbins till
they arrived at the police station.

"Good," said Scratch. "The cones are still here. All we have to do is push one pile down the pavement to the junction and..."

"Block off the other road," agreed Sniff. "That way the Doogood's van will have to come down the high street past the police station. But we must be quick, there's no time to lose."

The dogs hurried over to the nearest pile of cones.

"This will be easy," said Scratch. "When I was a champion sheep dog I was great at nudging sheep in the right direction."

"Then you can show me what to do," said Sniff. "I've only ever been a champion draught excluder."

Scratch nudged and pushed.

Sniff pushed and nudged.

Eventually the pile of cones reached the road junction. Then Sniff stepped off the pavement and held up a paw to stop the traffic, while Scratch toppled over the cones and lined them up across the road.

"Just look at those amazing dogs creating a diversion," said passers-by. "Whatever next!"

Scratch and Sniff hurried back to the police station. Penny was standing outside looking puzzled.

"There you are," she said. "I was wondering where you'd gone. Have you seen a pile of cones? I seem to have lost..."

Then she saw that all the cars in the high street had come to a halt.

"What's causing the traffic jam?" she wondered.

She was on her way to find out when she noticed the Doogood's van. "What's that doing here? Sergeant Snide shouldn't be allowing any vans to leave."

Scratch and Sniff looked at
each other.

"Well done, Penny!" they both
barked. "Good thinking!"

Chapter Four

Penny, followed by Scratch and Sniff, headed through the traffic jam to the Doogood's van.

The police constable rapped on the window.

"Can I have a word?" she said.

Bernie glanced at Stan, then rolled down the window.

"Certainly, Constable, how can I help you?"

"What are you carrying in your van?" asked Penny.

"Furniture," said Bernie. "See, it says so on the side of the van: DOOGOOD'S FURNITURE."

"That's the clue," giggled Stan.

"Could you open the back of your van, please?" said Penny. "I'd like to take a look."

"If you must, Constable," sighed Bernie. "But it's just furniture, and we're late for the delivery as it is."

Bernie and Stan got out and unlocked the back of the van.

"There you are," said Bernie.
"One three-seater sofa to be
delivered to Mrs Paterson,
4 Barnton Street."

Penny looked in the van. It was
completely empty apart from the sofa.
She climbed inside, walked all round
the sofa, then peered underneath.

"There certainly doesn't seem to be anything out of place," she frowned.

"Then we'll be on our way, Constable," said Bernie.

"As soon as you've cleared the traffic jam," added Stan.

Penny started to get out of the van so Scratch and Sniff had to act quickly.

"We need to let Penny know what's in that middle cushion or the robbers will get away!" barked Scratch.

Sniff nodded. "That sofa looks very comfortable," he said. "Fancy a lie-down?"

Chapter Five

Scratch jumped up onto the sofa.

Sniff jumped and got his front paws onto the sofa.

"The rest of me will be along shortly, Scratch," he panted, as his back legs scrabbled up behind him.

"What are you two doing?" cried Penny. "Get down this minute!"

"Yeah, clear off, mutts," muttered Bernie.

Scratch and Sniff ignored him
and lay down.

"Scratch! Sniff! You'll ruin
the sofa with your dirty paws!"
said Penny.

"Dirty paws?" said Scratch.
"Then we'd better clean them
hadn't we, Sniff?"

And she began to scrape away at the middle cushion.

Scrape. Scrape.

"Can't have dirty paws," agreed Sniff, and he joined in.

Scrape. Scrape.

Then they pushed the middle cushion onto the floor, and scraped at it again.

Scrape. Scrape.

"Control these dogs or we'll have the law on you, Constable," yelled Bernie and Stan.

"Be quiet!" said Penny. "I think the dogs are trying to tell me something..."

Scratch and Sniff looked at each other.

"The penny's dropped at last!" they barked.

Constable Penrose picked up the cushion and undid the back zip. Bundles of money fell out.

"Leg it, Stan!" cried Bernie. "The game's up!"

But Stan was already out of the van and running down the high street.

Bernie followed close behind.

"They're getting away!" cried Penny. "After them!"

Scratch bounded after Stan and pulled him down. **THUD! OW!**

Sniff bounded after Bernie and tripped him up. **THUD! OW!**

Penny caught up with them all. She grabbed Bernie and Stan.

"You're nicked," she grinned and marched them back to the police station.

Sergeant Snide arrived just as Penny was counting out the stolen money.

"What's that?" he demanded.

"The money from Doogood's furniture shop," grinned Penny. "Scratch and Sniff helped me to catch the robbers."

"And I'm taking Constable Penrose and the dogs to Mrs Pudding's cake shop to celebrate," said Inspector Hector.

Sergeant Snide glowered and stomped off.

"Congratulations on solving the case, Constable Penrose," said Inspector Hector, when they got to the cake shop.

"Thank you," replied Penny. "But the credit should really go to Scratch and Sniff."

The doggy Secret Service barked and wagged their tails. They liked solving problems and now they had another: which delicious cake should they choose?

"I feel like a sticky bun," decided Scratch.

"That's funny," said Sniff. "You look like a collie!"

READING ZONE!

WHAT DO YOU THINK?

Scratch and Sniff can speak to each other but they can't speak directly to the humans in the story.

Can you skim through the book and spot the different ways in which the dogs communicate with the humans to get what they want or the help they need?

READING ZONE!

QUIZ TIME

Can you remember the answers to these questions?

- What is Penny looking for at the start of the story?

- Where do Scratch and Sniff go for a 'proper meal'?

- Where does Bernie tell Stan he has stashed the money?

- What is Penny doing when Sergeant Snide returns to the police station?

- Which cake does Scratch choose as her reward?